Rocket
RIVALS

by
Lisa Harkrader

illustrated by Tammie Lyon

Kane Press
New York

For Larry, Ashley, and Austin,
who make life a blast.—L.H.

For Lee who can build just
about anything.—T.L.

Library of Congress Cataloging-in-Publication Data
Names: Harkrader, Lisa, author. | Lyon, Tammie, illustrator.
Title: Rocket rivals / by Lisa Harkrader ; illustrated by Tammie Lyon.
Description: New York : Kane Press, 2019. | Series: Makers make it work |
Summary: Erin is excited about the new Rocket Club at school, until she is paired with Lily, whose projects are always bright and glittery, for the final launch.
Identifiers: LCCN 2018022819 (print) | LCCN 2018029113 (ebook) | ISBN 9781635921205 (ebook) | ISBN 9781635921199 (pbk) | ISBN 9781635921182 (reinforced library binding)
Subjects: | CYAC: Competition (Psychology)—Fiction. | Rockets (Aeronautics)—Fiction. | Clubs—Fiction. | Schools—Fiction.
Classification: LCC PZ7.H22615 (ebook) | LCC PZ7.H22615 Roc 2019 (print) | DDC [E]—dc23
LC record available at https://lccn.loc.gov/2018022819

10 9 8 7 6 5 4 3 2 1

First published in the United States of America in 2019 by Kane Press, Inc.
Printed in China

Book Design: Michelle Martinez

Makers Make It Work is a registered trademark of Kane Press, Inc.

Visit us online at www.kanepress.com

 Like us on Facebook
facebook.com/kanepress

 Follow us on Twitter
@kanepress

Erin had a problem.

The problem's name was Lily.

Erin and Lily were in the same class. And whatever Erin did, Lily did bigger.

She did it brighter.

She did it with glitter and sparkly bows.

When their class made Egyptian pyramids, Erin did lots of research. She built an exact scale model of a pyramid. She dusted it with sand to make it look real.

Lily glued together crooked pieces of cardboard. She covered them with gold stars and beads.

"Very creative!" said their teacher, Ms. Kimura.
"It's as if the pharaoh's riches are spilling out."
"That's totally what I was going for," said Lily.
"Good work," said Ms. Kimura.
"Good grief," said Erin.

In gym class, Erin finished the mile run faster than anyone. Lily ran in rainbow knee socks. The class cheered her on.

The school held a pet show. Erin trained her dog to dance, shake hands, and take a bow. Lily dressed her dog in a tutu. She won first prize.

"I do the work. Lily gets the glory." Erin sighed. "I can't win."

Then Ms. Kimura passed out flyers for a new after-school club.

Erin read the flyer.

Want to
design a rocket?
Want to launch your rocket
and watch it fly?
Rocket Club
IS FOR YOU!

"All science. No glitter." Erin pressed the flyer
to her heart. "Rocket Club is for me!"

But when Erin walked into the first club meeting, guess who was in the front row. Lily.

"There's no glitter in rocketry," Erin told her.

Lily wrinkled her nose. "There should be."

Ms. Kimura started a movie. On the screen, astronauts entered a space capsule.

An announcer began counting.

"Three . . . two . . . one . . . liftoff!"

Erin held her breath.

The rocket rumbled. Smoke billowed. The rocket launched into the sky.

Arlo's eyes grew wide. "We're building that?"

Liftoff means the rocket shoots into the air.

"We'll start smaller." Ms. Kimura held up a plastic soda bottle. "We'll attach this to a launch tube. You stomp the bottle and force air through the tube and into the rocket. That's the thrust. When thrust is greater than the weight of the rocket, you get liftoff!"

Thrust is a force, or push, against the weight of the rocket.

Everyone rolled and glued sheets of paper to make the bodies of their rockets.

Erin glued a nose cone and fins on hers. She made everything smooth and straight. And airtight. If air leaked out when she stomped the bottle, her rocket wouldn't shoot as high.

And Erin wanted her rocket to shoot high.

The body of the rocket is also called the *fuselage*.

"Let's launch!" said Ms. Kimura. Rocket Club trooped outside.

Prisha's rocket shot above the school.

Arlo's shot above the flagpole.

It was Erin's turn.

"Three . . . two . . . one!" Rocket Club chanted.

Erin stomped. Her rocket shot above the trees.

"Whoooaaa!" cried Rocket Club.

Then it was Lily's turn. Her rocket was covered in shimmery gemstones.

"Oooooooo," murmured Rocket Club.

Lily stomped. Her rocket blooped from the launch tube. It flopped in the grass.

"Too much drag," said Ms. Kimura. "But our next rockets will take more time. They'll have parachutes so they float down after the launch."

Parachutes! Erin smiled.

Drag is a force that pulls on something, making it hard to move. Lily's gemstones are bumpy. Air can't move smoothly over a bumpy rocket. The bumps increase the drag on the rocket.

Erin spent days building her rocket. She practiced folding her parachute and tucking it inside. She slid the nose cone on, straight and snug.

On launch day, Leonard went first. His parachute didn't open.

Rosie's opened, but the strings got tangled.

Erin slid her rocket onto the launcher. She stomped.

Whoooosh! The rocket shot to the sky.

Pop! The parachute burst out. Rocket and parachute floated to the ground.

Erin's heart swelled. It worked!

Then it was Lily's turn.

Lily's rocket was smooth. But her fins were stars with ribbons.

She stomped. Her rocket shot up—

—and crashed to the ground.

Lily picked up a ribbon. "The decorations fell off!"

"Fins aren't decorations," said Ms. Kimura. "They give the rocket stability. You'll need lots of stability for our final project. Our rockets will carry cargo. An egg."

Erin blinked. An *egg*!

"It must land without a crack," Ms. Kimura said. "We'll work in pairs. Arlo and Prisha. Rosie and Leonard. Erin and—"

Stability means the rocket is steady. It flies straight and doesn't wobble.

Another word for the cargo a rocket carries is *payload*.

"—Lily," said Ms. Kimura.

Lily? Erin's mouth dropped open.

"How lucky is this?" Lily squeezed up next to Erin. "Your genius rocket skills. My sense of style. We're the perfect pair."

Erin began researching rocket designs. "We'll put the egg close to the nose cone," she told Lily. "For stability."

"Let's *paint* the nose cone," said Lily.

Erin tested ways to cushion the egg. "We can't let it bounce around."

"I know! We'll use glitter paint!" said Lily.

Erin gritted her teeth.

"We're supposed to be partners," Erin told Lily. "But I do all the work. What do you add? *Glitter.*"

Lily's chin trembled. "I'm not like you. I can't make a perfect Egyptian pyramid. I can't train a perfect dog. I sure can't build a perfect rocket. I can't do anything perfect."

Erin swallowed. She hadn't meant to hurt Lily's feelings. "You glue perfectly."

"I've had lots of practice gluing glitter," Lily said.

"It's settled." Erin smiled. "You can be Chief of Gluing."

Erin and Lily built their rocket. They practiced dropping it from the top of the bleachers. The parachute opened. The rocket floated down. The egg broke.

Every time.

"It comes down too fast," said Erin.

"Too bad we can't have drag," said Lily. "That sure slowed down my rocket."

"We do have drag," said Erin. "The parachute."

"Maybe we need more," said Lily.

Erin stared at her. "Lily," she said, "you're a genius."

Erin and Lily set to work once again. Erin designed. Lily glued. Lily had ideas. Erin listened. Finally, launch day arrived.

Arlo and Prisha's rocket shot to the sky. But their egg cracked.

Rosie and Leonard's egg landed safely. But their rocket flew barely as high as the swing set.

Ms. Kimura turned to Erin and Lily. "Ready?"

Erin placed their rocket on the launch tube. Lily set up their sound system.

"Three . . . two . . . one . . ."

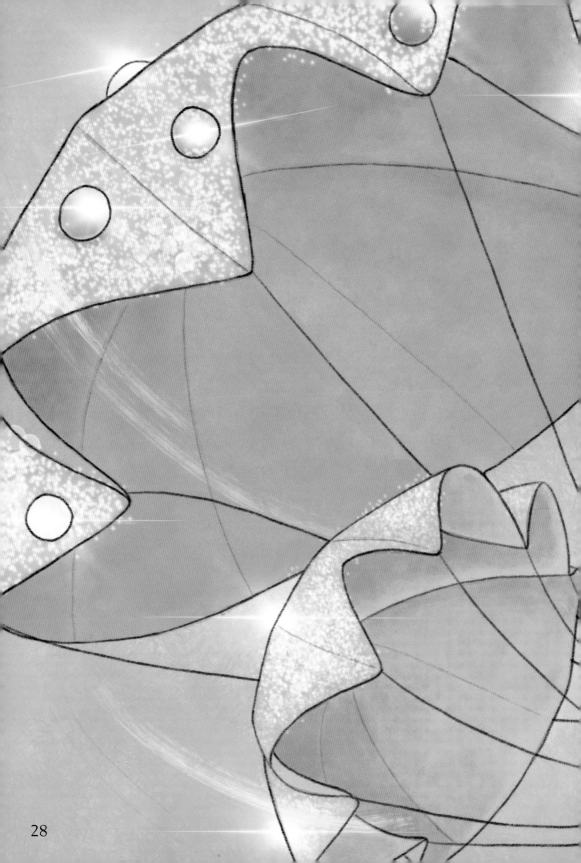

Erin stomped. Lily pressed PLAY.

Whooooosh! The rocket shot to the sky.

Da-dum! Music blasted through the air.

Pop! The parachute burst out. Its dazzling colors shimmered in the sun.

"Oooooo!" murmured Rocket Club.

Pop! A second parachute spread out above the first.

"COOOOOOL!" cried Rocket Club.

The rocket floated to the ground.

Erin held her breath. Ms. Kimura pulled out the egg. She checked it front and back.

"Not a crack," Ms. Kimura said. "Excellent work."

Erin whooped. Lily cheered.

"Erin came up with the design," Lily said.

Erin put her arm around her new friend. "And Lily made it shine."

Learn Like a Maker

Rocket design is not as simple as 1, 2, 3. Erin thought about the fuselage, nose cone, parachute, and fins. She improved her design with each launch test . . . and even improved her friendship with Lily!

Look Back

- ✖ On page 7, Erin says, "I do the work. Lily gets the glory." How is Erin feeling at this point? Have you ever felt that way?

- ✖ Reread page 12. Why do you think it's important for air to not leak out of the rocket?

Try This!

Build a Rocket

What you need:

- ✖ 1 index card
- ✖ Markers
- ✖ Scissors
- ✖ Masking tape
- ✖ 2 different size straws (1 slightly larger in diameter than the other)

1. On the index card, draw a picture of a rocket and cut it out.
2. Cut off a 4-inch-long piece of the larger straw. Tape over one end to seal it.
3. Tape the straw to the back of the picture, with the sealed part at the rocket's top end.
4. Slide the second straw into the rocket straw.
5. Point the rocket away from any people and blow into the straw. Be careful not to hold onto the rocket.

Watch your rocket fly!